QUEST OF A BIPOLAR SOLDIER

QUEST OF A BIPOLAR SOLDIER

BY

WINSTON K. REDMAN

Published by
Bookstand Publishing
Morgan Hill, CA 95037
4248_2

Copyright © 2015 by Winston K. Redman
All rights reserved. No part of this publication may be reproduced or transmitted in any form or by any means, electronic or mechanical, including photocopy, recording, or any information storage and retrieval system, without permission in writing from the copyright owner.

ISBN 978-1-63498-076-6

Printed in the United States of America

I DEDICATE THIS BOOK TO ALL THOSE WHO ARE AT WAR WITH MENTAL ILLNESS AND DRUG ADDICTION. ALSO TO ALL THOSE FAMILIES WHO HAVE LOST ANYONE IN THIS GREAT AND ONGOING BATTLE.

CONTENTS

Chapter 1: 1985, the 2nd Day of October: When I, KOS, Landed Here on Planet Earth or Should I Just Simply Say the Day on Which I was Born.. 1

Chapter 2: Chaotic Episode Sets in: Where I Lost Touch with Reality 7

Chapter 3: The Beginning of My Insanity 11

Chapter 4: Failure of Intervention... 15

Chapter 5: Intervention Continues in Failure... 17

Chapter 6: Back to the House of God 21

Chapter 7: Back to Running the Streets.. 25

Chapter 8: Pain of the Great Deception 29

Chapter 9: "Close Your Eyes and Look Around You" 33

Chapter 10: Back to K-Town... 37

Chapter 11: Near-Death Experience 41

Chapter 12: Zombie Land 47

Chapter 13: New Place 51

Chapter 14: Peggy and Our Journey Together.. 55

Chapter 15: Will It Ever End? 59

Chapter 16: Vain Game of Stupidity Continues to Remain 67

Chapter 17: Tryin' to Focus... 71

Chapter 18: Will I Ever Make It Back? 75

Chapter 19: High-Speed Chase 83

Chapter 20: Last Chance... 87

Chapter 21: "Lord, I Don't Wanna Die Like This" 91

Chapter 22: Retaliation that Happened 95

Chapter 23: Is This The End? 99

CHAPTER 1
1985, THE 2ND DAY OF OCTOBER: WHEN I, KOS, LANDED HERE ON PLANET EARTH OR SHOULD I JUST SIMPLY SAY THE DAY IN WHICH I WAS BORN

I was born in Germany into a military family. At first it was just me, mom, dad, and older sister; until cry baby sissy pants came along, my little brother Zay. For about another seven years it was just the five of us. We lived in El Paso, Texas, while my dad was stationed at Fort Bliss. I remember times, when I was about three, riding around in armored tanks and also at times running around and playing with the neighborhood kids.

One day, I had gotten a fresh pair of kicks; my mom had bought me Nikes to be exact. We were pretty poor and my mom getting those shoes was like buying a new bike; she told me to take care of them. I wanted to show them off, so I went to the house of a kid where there was a blue kid's pool that had what I believe to be fish designs all around it. While there I had to take my shoes off to get into the water.

While I was in the pool this neighborhood bully took my shoes. I told him to give them back, and he then threw them onto the roof of a building and told me to get them myself.

I began to get a little scared, knowing how mom would react and not wanting to tell her; and I was afraid that the kid bully might beat me up later on down the road.

When I got home mom kept asking me, "What happened to your new shoes?" until I finally told her.

Then me and mom went to the kid bully's house and spoke to his mom, and she made the kid get on a ladder and get my shoes. He said only one he could find, however, so one was all I got back. I guess this is when I began to realize there would be many difficult situations on the road ahead of me.

Years passed, and I was living in Fort Knox, Kentucky. This was where my baby brother, B-chan, was born. I was in church at the time and had taken my religion very seriously. I attended a Pentecostal church, where I was baptized in the name of Jesus Christ at age nine.

At age 10 I was laying in my bed, praying to the Lord for the Holy Ghost, when I was filled and came forth speaking in tongues, which is the sign of being filled with the spirit of Jesus Christ.

I walked how I was supposed to walk for a while. My friends respected me and would not say a curse word, and if such a word slipped out they would apologize. I remember one time my friend Michael felt like cussing, so he told me I should walk the other way home after school. For him to do that really made me think and ask, "Can't you just not cuss?"

He replied, "Kos, just go home."

Kentucky was the favorite place I lived because of the church and the friends I had who respected me for who I was.

I soon moved back to Germany, where my dad had been stationed once again. Problems started to come into my life, and I wasn't well prepared spiritually or mentally to deal with them.

I would go to school and kids would always make fun of how I dressed, asking, "Why does everyone else in your family dress nice, but you dress like a clown?" That's when what I wore on my body began to matter for the wrong reasons. To look "cool" and impress people whose thoughts or opinions shouldn't have mattered, I started to get into fights. I would even steal, if I thought I could get away with it, to feed my addiction to German candy. Sounds funny, but this was really the beginning of what would lead up to the rest of my problems in my future.

My dad was a football coach, so he moved me to a different school so I could learn from watching the high school football team play. I would help by being the ball boy on the sidelines, making sure the ball was always dry, especially on rainy and snowy days.

I wound up getting into trouble for setting a house on fire that was in a German neighborhood. My friend Q and I wound up setting the house on fire from the bottom to top, back to the bottom. People say we were lucky to get out alive, being that we started the fire at the bottom of the house, went to the top and started more fire, then had to go back through where we had started the fire to get back out. I say that God had His angel watching over us. As punishment we had to perform 200 hours of community service ordered by a Colonel, and we were warned that if we got into any more trouble we would have to go back to the States.

I kept getting into trouble for being too talkative in class or disrespecting the teacher. I remember getting beat for a whole school year until I wound up getting sent to live with my grandmother, Molly. I continued getting in trouble while staying with her, and had to move to Vikingsburg.

I had to go to church at least once a week. However, I really didn't take heed of what was being said there; it would go in one ear and out the other. I would just worry about things like women and the 21 and Under Club, where I had met this 21-year-old girl named Joni when I was 13. She was the first whom I had sex with. Now, being older, I find it inappropriate behavior for a 21-year-old to have sex with someone 13.

I couldn't stay out of trouble in school, so me, my mom, my brothers, and my sister moved back to West Virginia, because I was too much for my cousins to handle. We moved to Tornadoville, West Virginia.

This is the point in my life when drugs and alcohol hit me and took almost complete control over my mind. I would smoke weed and drink, mainly on the weekends. I would go to school dances, and bum dollars, until I had enough to buy a $20 bag of weed.

I would drink alcohol and smoke weed, and I thought that marijuana took care of every problem that I was facing, which was a total and complete lie to myself.

For truancy I got sent off to the Salem Industrial Home for Youth. I went under a 30-day diagnostic observation. After the 30 days, I appeared back in front of the courts, and it was there that I was deemed not fit to return back to the public. Instead, was sent to an all-boys private school, Wood Ridge, which was more like a boot camp.

I ran away from this place many times and never got caught, but I always wound up turning myself in. I would rebel against any staff member who would try and direct me into the way I was supposed to go. I would get restrained by two staff members, one sitting on my back and the other one on my buttocks for hours at times. My trouble never seemed to decrease, but would go on until they sent me away to another juvenile facility, which was temporary; then I had to return to this school.

I began to get my act together. I played football, and worked in the dining hall washing dishes all day for a high school credit and $2.25 an hour.

CHAPTER 2

CHAOTIC EPISODE SETS IN: WHERE I LOST TOUCH WITH REALITY

The summer before my 10th grade year was about over. Football practice had begun, but I was not so aware of what was happening, and I was beginning to lash out at my fellow peers. I would threaten them, thinking they were all out to get me. My mind was slipping away from me, as I was beginning to enter into a state of psychosis.

It so happened that I would stop sleeping for days. I started to think the staff was going to kill me. I would go AWOL from my unit at the school, thinking that the world was coming to an end. At one point this staff member came to me and tried to talk to me, wondering what was wrong with me. I was so far gone that I asked him if the moon was the sun, thinking that Armageddon had begun. I started to believe I was King David back from the dead. Then I thought I was the Anti-Christ.

I wound up getting put up in a psych ward in Virginia. They kept me there for three weeks, then released me back into the custody of the Wood Ridge all-boys private school. I was okay for about a week, and then I started to lose it again. My coach talked to me about playing football, but I told him I was not going to play; I couldn't even really focus on what we were talking about. He tried to tell me that if I played he would allow me to pick whatever position I wanted. But he couldn't get me to play — and that was the end of my dreams to be a professional athlete.

I wound up going back to the psych ward in Virginia. I would watch TV and think I was the characters in the movies and programs I watched. Eventually I was in such bad shape that I was put in seclusion, or what some would think of as a padded room. I thought I was seeing people who weren't there, and I thought I saw angels. I would think some of the craziest thoughts. I even thought I was Peter Pan and could fly.

I wound up getting sent to Charleston, West Virginia, to Highland Hospital, which is now the old Highland Hospital. I was there for about 30 days. While there I began to get a grip on reality, and was released by the hospital into the custody of the sheriff, who transported me to a group home in Romney, West Virginia, because my probation officer wanted me housed in a long-term facility. She didn't feel like the group home was a safe environment for me.

In all reality, she just wanted to try and make me suffer; she hated kids, regardless of their shapes, sizes, and colors. I wound up the next day being transported to the South Central Regional Juvenile Detention Center (SCRJDC). However, they said they couldn't keep me because of the simple fact that I had no recent charges or convictions and was not awaiting trial. So they sent me back to the group home in Romney, and I thought I was good to go.

But it so happened that the next day I was picked up and taken back to SCRJDC, and waited for them to find for me a place that would accept me with my mental illness. I spent two-and-a-half months at SCRJDC, most of my time spent in a cell. I met people who were in there for many different reasons: Murders, grand theft auto, burglary, and so on and so forth.

Finally, they found a place in Columbia, South Carolina, where I met a lot of amazing people who really did their best to lead me in the right direction. Two individuals in particular, Mr. Edward (who we called Mr. E) and Mr. Goodin, inspired me to pursue my Rap career, which I'm still pursuing to this day.

Mr. Leon, an ex-semipro ball player, was another individual I found myself looking up to. In a way he made me think about my addiction to marijuana, and I thought to myself, *If he could go without smoking and still have a good time, I could do the same.* I wish I would have always reminded myself of that thought.

My peers looked up to me as a leader, and I was voted President of the group which was held weekly and would give advice about things.

One guy I thought I would never be friends with was Renee. We fought all the time when I first got there, and I wound up gaining his respect. One day, however, he made me mad and I said something to him that haunts me to this day, something I would rather keep out of this book. It hurt him pretty bad. I wish he knew how sorry I am for that.

I wound up completing the program faster than anyone had ever completed it, and with the fewest write-ups. I have mentioned a few people who made an impact on my life there, but it wasn't just them who impacted my life — it was actually everyone who was there.

My day of release came, and my mom, dad, and little brother came to pick me up. After that I never thought I'd be in, or ever put myself in, a situation that would place me in such circumstances again.

CHAPTER 3
THE BEGINNING OF MY INSANITY

Up to this point everyone was wondering what had gone wrong in my head. I would like to say it is possible that I was screwed up in the head from the beginning, back when I was in Texas at age three. I believe I felt a bit lonesome. I remember spending time in my room alone trying to make friends with the dust particles floating around in the sun rays that shot forth through my window.

There's a day I remember when my dad came home after a baseball game in El Paso, Texas, when I was still three. He was drunk and bloody from a fight he had gotten into with someone at the game. My mom was trying to keep him out of the house and his soldier buddies were trying to hold him back. My mom then told us we were leaving; I was wondering if it was for good. At that age, you don't really understand much that goes on and you try to figure out what is going on. Anyway, we wound up going out the back door and staying with some of my mom's friends for a few hours.

We did eventually go back home. My mom, later on in years when I would bring up that day, would talk about how my dad was sitting on the bed saying nobody loved him but his dog. Sometimes I wonder if he knows I always loved him even when he was ignorantly minded about things towards me.

Around age five, I remember being left alone in my dad's car in the middle of the night, for hours. He and his army buddies went up into someone's apartment doing, whatever, when we were supposed to be going to the movies. I was left in the car for so long that the car ran out of gas and shut off.

When my dad finally returned to the car, he told me he was sorry and had forgotten that I was in there, and he told me not to tell my mom.

Many times after this, I remember spending time in the car while my dad would be in some buddy's house. He said he was talking to their wives about important things going on, and I'm not exactly sure what was really going on. But I have ideas.

My sister, brother, and I once went to Burger King and we began to flick ice back and forth. My dad had told us to stop, and I did, but my sister and brother did not. I was five, my brother three, and my sister seven. My dad said we were going to get a beating when we got home.

I said, "Dad, I quit when you said."

But he just said, "You and your sister are getting it when you get home."

The whole way home I begged him not to and said, "I didn't do it."

He said, "If you didn't do it, God won't let you feel the pain when I beat you."

I started to pray. Then we got beat with a belt until I lied and said, "Okay, I did it."

He said, "Now you're lying," and he hit me with the belt again for lying, and I felt the pain. Of course, after I said I did it, my sister, as weird as she can be sometimes, tried to say she did it, which was true. My dad was like, "It's too late, you should have come forth before your brother," and he beat her a good one.

There were times that I would get picked on by other kids. This one kid pulled my hair when I had long hair. I would tell my dad and mom, and I really didn't know much about fighting. They told me to stand up for myself; if they pulled my hair, I was to pull their hair back and even start hitting them. I realize now that this is not proper or appropriate behavior for any parent to teach their children. I started fighting all the time, and I even learned a little martial arts.

The stress I had in my head led me to become a very angry child and hating my life. At an early age my family one day went somewhere, and I didn't go, and for some reason I was highly irritated and clawed my face, leaving four claw marks down the side of my face.

My parents just thought I was being spoiled, when really I think that was the beginning of my insanity.

CHAPTER 4
FAILURE OF INTERVENTION

I finally got my freedom after two and half years of incarceration. With no hesitation, I found myself back with my old friends B, Cain, and Stilts. I met up with them on my second day out. While we were walking down the street a blunt was sparked and I was back to smoking with the homies.

Everything had changed in those two and a half years; weed wasn't the only drug being used anymore. Things had gotten a lot worse. I heard of Oxycontin for the first time, I came to know it as being synthetic heroin. My cousin B, Lee, and Cain found this drug to be one they were trying to escape as well as heroin and cocaine. I saw more heroin in B and Lee's room one time at age 16 than I have ever seen in my whole life.

I tried to just stick to smoking weed and drinking. There was a teacher at the high school who would send my cousin home with bags full of Northern Lights, a high-grade bud. That took you even higher than swag or dirt weed or mid-grade. The first time I smoked it I started drooling.

I started working at a telemarketing service, which was a place full of drug addicts. I would leave and go smoke, come back, and could barely talk to the clients on the other line. My bosses would tell me to go home and come back sober, because I was an excellent salesman when I wasn't high.

I met up with this guy named Romeo, and we would go to his house and smoke and drink. One night I was introduced to cocaine by his friend from Petersburg. I used to tell people I had heart problems so they wouldn't try to peer-pressure me into using cocaine. But this night I was drunk and gave in on the third time it was offered; alcohol does definitely cause poor judgment.

A time came when Stilts and I would get together every day to find bud to smoke. We would usually go to our friends, Slick and Snake, and chill all day.

CHAPTER 5
INTERVENTION CONTINUES IN FAILURE

New Year's 2002; Snake, Slick, Jeff, and I got together. Jeff was a friend from school, and we wound up going to the Projects and drank all night. I lost count of how many beers I drank. After a while my cousin Jay came up a little before the ball dropped and sparked up a blunt right at 12:00 midnight. I took some shots of Seagram Seven, and one of my friends asked if I was all right and I said, "My nose is bleeding." As things began to fade out, I still said I was all right.

Then I had a blackout and the next day woke up at home, not knowing how I got there. My little brother and my friend, Wease, was there the night I came home. They didn't tell me what happened, and neither did my sister. She just asked me if I wanted to go eat at Denny's. I told her I didn't have any money, and she said she would pay for it. I didn't even have a hangover or anything.

While at Denny's I saw that my friend Mighty Mouse was there. I asked him what had happened, because we all usually chilled at Snake and Slick's together. He said, "You don't remember? You almost died." He went on to tell me that I was throwing up blood and bleeding from the nose. Later on I found out that everyone, but my cousin Jay and friends Slick and Jeff, had left me for dead. Jay called my mom, and Jeff and Slick helped get me into the car. My mom said she had to stay up all night with me to make sure I stayed on my side, because I kept turning over on my back and would have drowned in my own vomit if she hadn't done so. I continued to get high, but let up on the alcohol at this point in my life.

    I had dropped out of high school, and on some Friday nights I would go to this 21 and under club called Phat Rabbitz. My friend Lil' Mickey, whom I'd met at the alternative school, wound up chillin' with me all the time. We would go to Phat Rabbitz.

    One night I met this girl and tried to get her back to my house. We got a ride halfway back to my house from C-land. Lil' Mickey, her, and I got stuck at this drunk fest. I was just trying to find some weed to smoke there the whole night, but could only find beer; and drank it only because I was thirsty. Lil' Mickey, the girl from C-land and I kept trying to find a ride because the ride we'd had left us.

    We wound up having to walk, and we walked about five miles. Stopping at this house, we called someone to come pick us up, and as we walked on they met us. I got the girl back to my house, but I didn't get what I was working on the whole night, and she wound up calling her friends and they picked her up from my house.

I wasn't doing good for myself, so it got to the point where I went to live with my dad in Leesville, Louisiana. I was staying in the hood where it wasn't cool to wear certain colors unless you were well known. I stayed there for about three weeks and wound up losing my mind. I went into a psychological relapse.

It so happened that I didn't have a constant supply of weed, which I was using to self-medicate, and in all reality I was trying to quit. I was working at this place called Daylight Donuts at the time, and I started thinking that the radio was talking about me. One time, when it was talking about a bad wreck, I was so delirious I thought I was involved in the wreck and had died.

I then started seeing things. I thought I saw a rabbit hopping under the counter I made the donuts on. Immediately I began to pray to the Lord, asking Him not to let this happen to me again.

But it was too late; it had already begun. I left the donut shop looking for churches that would let me in to pray. My dad didn't' know what to do with me, so he took me to the hospital to try and get help, but they wouldn't give me the help I needed. He would talk to my mom saying stuff like, "What if it isn't Kos that's crazy? What if we're the crazy ones?"

She told him to get me home, so we went on a three-day trip back to K-town.

Mom wound up taking me to C-land and had me admitted to the hospital's psych ward. After three days I convinced the doctor to let me go. I still was not in the right mind, though, and why he let me go, I don't know.

I started going back to church every Friday, Sunday, and Wednesday. I would act kind of crazy in church, thinking I was the Messiah.

Mom wound up taking me back to the hospital, and she got my cousin John to come with her. They wound up taking me back to C-land, and I began to get a bit aggressive there and the staff sedated me and had me taken by ambulance to a place in H-town. They wound up keeping me until I came back to earth instead of wandering around in space or Wonderland like Alice or the Mad Hatter.

CHAPTER 6
BACK TO THE HOUSE OF GOD

Now here I am about 18 years old. After years of chaotic episodes, one after another, I found myself back in church praying and giving God the praise He deserves. My family and I would attend every Wednesday, Friday, Sunday morning, and Sunday night.

My dad, who was in Fort Polk, Louisiana, wound up moving back home to K-town. He also began to attend church services. It seemed he was one way at church and then another way at home. I would go to work, come home, and go to church, and I remained sober for the time I was back to going.

It so happened that seemingly nothing I did could ever please my dad or make him proud of me. At church, after I would rise to share a testimony, he would say things like, "This is the first time I ever been able to witness you as a man."

But as soon as we would return home, there would be unnecessary complaining about a lot of small things like eating, and showering too much; he even had the fridge locked with a chain even when I would buy my own food. Also at this time, if I recall, I was only 195–200 lbs. He would also make fun of a girlfriend I had at the time. While we would be sitting at a church dinner, he would be behind me, making fun behind my back, making a gesture to his cousin that she batted left and right. He would do things to humiliate me in a childlike manner.

Actually, I'm kind of glad because it caused me not to stay with her. I really was trying to do right by God, and she, I know, would not have allowed me to do so. Not by her intentions, of course, but just by the effect some women have on men when they are trying to do the right thing. I soon wound up meeting this other young lady from another church, who I saw as beautiful, and for some reason I saw her as being too good for me.

We began talking by her approaching me one day at church. As we talked we shared things that we wanted in our future, things like cars and such. I made a mistake one day in my belief if it was not made I would be living a good life and possibly with her.

It came to be that one day after work I was headed to my sister's; then from there I was to go to church. But in my path came temptation, temptation into which I fell in the belief that my stress would be taken away. This temptation was in the form of two of my old friends who were smoking a joint. Knowingly I asked them, "What are you doing?"

They replied, "Smoking a joint. You want to hit it?"

I thought to myself, *Well, I have been stressing a lot.* With that I then took hold of the J and puffed, inhaled, breathing in condemnation. I then walked away and the buzz soon kicked in.

Suddenly "God" crossed my mind. I was overtaken by shame and felt like hiding such as when Adam and Eve did when they ate of the forbidden tree. I ended up not going to church on that occasion because I felt like I was the worst person in the world. Maybe it was because I would judge the ones in church whom I knew chewed tobacco or smoked or even drank. The finger I pointed at others strongly and fiercely pointed three-fold back at me. By my words I was justified and by my words I was condemned.

At the time I was supposed to go to church that night, I stayed at my sister's with my brother Zay instead. When my sister and mom came home they said, "You should've went, Kos! Sarah was there asking about you." If there's anything I regret it was the two things that occurred that day: My smoking, and my not going to church and realizing that life is a process of growing.

That I came to find out none too soon.

Four years went by and my sister told me that the young lady I had seen as beautiful, the one who had approached me four years earlier and whom I only got to share a moment of my dreams with, still asked about me. To this day I wonder what would have happened if I had gone to church that night. But I do realize that everything happens for good for those who love God and are the called according to His purpose.

CHAPTER 7
BACK TO RUNNING THE STREETS

After not going back to church, and smoking that joint, it wasn't long before I hooked up with an old so-called friend, Snake. I started going to Snake's house and would smoke with him and his girlfriend. One day, not knowing that he was into big-time dealing, I asked him if he knew where I could find a dime. He said, "I don't know, maybe." Then he went into his kitchen and said, "Is this straight?" I was kind of amazed at the amount he returned with; it wasn't your usual one blunt dime, it was 3.5 grams, what I used to get for $20.00.

After I went to his house a few more times, he asked if I wanted to start moving for him. I said, "Sure."

He was like, "How much can you handle? How about I start you off with one or two ounces, charging a hundred an O?"

So I hit the streets again, this time looking for customers. I didn't stop 'till I found people who liked smoking.

I walked by this garage around 9:30 or so at night. Seeing the lights on and hearing people talking I knew they were smoking because with their talking I heard coughing.

I met this dude Neff, who became my first customer; I asked if he knew anyone looking. He bought some that night with his friend in the background yelling, "Don't do it! He's a cop!"

I said, "Do I really look like a cop? If I was I wouldn't be trying to sell bud."

Neff happened to know I was the real deal. He bought and asked for my number, and that's how it all started.

The next time I went to re-up I got another 2-oninos and got rid of them in less than 15 minutes. Went to re-up, again, and Snake said, "I never seen anybody move it that quick. You wanna try a QP?" That is four ounces, and it was gone the next day. I brought him $400.00 and had about $180.00 to spend and some to smoke. I started to think, *This is it. I'm going to be the biggest dealer talked about for years to come.* A dream so vain.

The day I went to re-up on the QP, Snake asked me if I wanted to see something. I was like, "Of course." People would always talk about how much tree this person or that person had. I was always like, "Yeah, right," like it was a really a big deal to see a large amount of weed. But that day he showed me four duffle bags that carried between 15 and 20 pounds. As he showed me he said, "You ready to take it to the next level?" It should be obvious what I said in reply — and I then went from moving ounces to moving pounds.

I would front a few people trying to keep family out listening to Big's Ten Crack Commandments; money and blood don't mix. I was moving bud, having the whole town on so-called lock.

I worked at Mickey D's to throw the cops off, though they were being paid off by the bosses above me. By keeping their pockets straight it kept the weed flowing. The ones who were really the ones to look out for were the Feds. While working at Mickey D's I had it made. Three other pushers worked with me: Mighty Mouse, Malli Mal, and the manager. We would rarely work while high, as there could have been a lot of complaints from customers such as, "There's a bite out of my hamburger," or, "I ordered a six-piece McNugget, not two."

Though I didn't smoke at work, I would bring work to work. To me there was always time to make money, and if I could make some extra, why not? If Malli Mal or Mighty Mouse weren't working, I would then have the manager watch the grill while one of my personal customers would come in.

It wasn't long before the ladies started throwing themselves in my path. I started going to the house of one of my brother's friends, who had three sisters who were lovely to the eye. But the one I chose was not so kind to my heart. Her name was Dellilah, and she told her brother she liked me. The crazy thing is that night me and my cousin B were going to go there, and I found out she liked me and I was going to go for this mixed chick who had a crush on me from way back, and, well, B was supposed to go for Dellilah. It didn't work out that way. I hooked up with Dellilah and B went home before she got there, after smoking a blunt with me.

Dellilah was the third person I'd been with. There were nights that would last till morning. I'd have to say that I couldn't wear her out, but I slept good. I remember one night I was so drained I almost fell asleep while hitting it from the back.

So stupid I was that I wound up buying a car for her. I bought it off my dope dealer for a grand. We didn't put any oil in it after I did a lot of traveling back and forth to Stilt's house, and the car blew a gasket.

CHAPTER 8
PAIN OF THE GREAT DECEPTION

A little while before I purchased the car, Snake wanted me to move in with him and his girlfriend. He wanted me to start handling the duffle bags. He was also trying to get me away from Dellilah because he saw her as bad news, which she was. He even told me that if I didn't cut her off, well, he was going to have to cut me off till I got my head back on my shoulders. He said I wasn't the same person. Which was true: I got some and went crazy. I guess women can have that bad effect on men even when the men are doing the wrong thing.

It was thus that I got cut off from him fronting me anymore. Dellilah and I happened to go a different route. We started getting fronted from some Jamaican she knew and probably blew. I was blinded by her outside appearance, and I thought she was all that mattered. She began to say things like, "Kos, are you burning, 'cause if you're burning I'm burning." I didn't think I was burning, but she burnt me. I didn't know until we broke up and I wound up getting some from this girl at her sister's house. I noticed a bump but I thought it was a cyst because it looked like ones I had used to get on my leg. After I was with that chick at Dellila's sister's, I went to a medical clinic because something just wasn't right. It turned out I had to change the name of my anaconda to Herp Worm Slim.

The day Dellilah and I broke up, she was giving me a ride back up to my parents' house. We wound up getting stopped by the police. The night before she so happened to hit a car and ran, and didn't even tell me. The tags on the car were from the other car that I had bought. I wasn't thinking smart at all and so happened to be riding dirty. I had two ounces in my pocket I had to hurry up and stuff in my shoe. The cop wound up searching the car. I forgot about this blunt I had rolled up in my book bag, and he wound up finding it. I just got a fine for it and for switching the car tags. He never searched me to see if I had more. Thank God! I had been about to bolt, but didn't.

It so happened that I didn't make it back to the house and went back to hers. While there, these three dudes came in and robbed me; one said he had a gun under his shirt. Even if that wasn't so, I couldn't have taken the three of them. They only got me for an ounce, though I had one stashed in each sock and a QP locked up in a gun case. For years I was wanting to get back at the one who said he had a gun, but didn't. He wound up going to prison. When he got out, I was going to put it to him, which I'll get to later. My other homies wound up putting the burner to him and took him for everything, but that's another story.

Soon after, I wound up back at my parents'. I ended up getting in a fight with my dad because I just couldn't take him anymore. I wound up pointing a berretta 9mm replica at him while he was on the phone with the dispatcher, yelling, "He's got a gun! He's got a gun!"

I just went into my room, gathered some clothes, put the gun back in my drawer, and my mom took me to talk to my pastor.

I called the police to see if they had a warrant on me, and they didn't. I never went back to living at home again. My dad caused nerve damage in my left shoulder. Me and my lil' homie Q wound up chillin'. He was on the run from the 5-0; we would sleep in my broken-down ride that was up the alley from Dellilah's house.

Winston K. Redman

CHAPTER 9
"CLOSE YOUR EYES AND LOOK AROUND YOU"

My dad had driven me and my brother out of the house. My dad tried beating up my brother one day, and Zay wound up hitting him in the head with a 2x4. Both of us were just running the streets, my brother being 16 and me 18. My mom decided to intervene and took us down to live with her sister in the Cacalacis.

Before that occurred I wound up losing my mind and ended up going to jail. I was delusional and hallucinating badly. While sitting in the cell I thought I was in hell. I believed there were snake eggs in my head and that they were going to hatch and eat me from the inside out. I thought that I was really in a train of some sort that moved from state to state, trading prisoners for money. I even thought I was down in a Mexican prison. Maybe that was the result of seeing a lot of Mexicans come in there. I would holler and try fighting the guards, which didn't work out too well. They would strap me to this chair; then, after a while, they would just throw me back in the cell. I started hearing snake rattles and thought snakes were going to drop out the ceiling, I even thought there were snakes in my pillows and thought the C.O.'s were a big part of organized crime and had dead bodies ground into pieces of dust and stuffed into the mattresses. I thought all kinds of crazy stuff and didn't have the slightest clue as to what was going on with me.

After my going two weeks with no sleep, they finally did a mental hygiene on me and I wound up in the looney bin. Then, it so happened, they released me illegally into the custody of my mom — illegally because I wasn't stable at the time. My brothers, sister, mom, and I went to live with my aunt, uncle, and cousins. I was still in a state of mania and not sleeping, however, and so my uncle would slip me a pill to knock me out but I would wake up with agitation. My mom would give me money so I could get some weed because it seemed like the only thing that would chill me out.

I wound up giving my cousin three of my Klonopin tablets one day, and afterwards he attempted to drive back to his house and almost got into a wreck. He was so high that he got pulled over and went to jail. I thought I was Melchizedek or the King of Salem, and that Jesus was not a person but a people that was hung on a tree.

My uncle and I became pretty close. He would talk to me and would try and get me calmed down. We would be out on the back porch, and he would have me stand in the middle of the yard and have me spin in circles. He would say, "Close your eyes and look around you. Then open them. One day you will understand why I have you doing this."

Now, after having spent four years incarcerated, I think I finally figured why he had me do this. My aunt told me she opened the bathroom door and my uncle was in there, crying because of me. He couldn't take it too much longer, so he told my mom we had to leave.

The day before we were supposed to go back to K-town I got arrested for driving 95 mph in a 55-mph zone after taking my mom's car. I was thinking about suicide, but decided not to do it. I wound up back in jail for 30 days. At first they had me in this cell that was covered with ants. I was hearing voices badly. I thought I heard other people's voices that weren't there — whose voices I cannot remember.

I wouldn't eat; and I went along thinking I was God. It so happened that I would think I had the last say on who went to hell. I had this vision, when I looked in the mirror in the cell, that my eyes and mouth had blue flames of fire coming out of them.

The day came that they let me out of the cell and put me in population, and I saw a picture of a face someone had drawn that resembled the same vision I'd had except that the face in the picture had scars on it. I asked one of the inmates, "Who drew that?" He said someone he knew had drawn it more than a year earlier. I told him about the dream I had, but he didn't believe me.

Eventually, I got thrown back into the hole for threatening inmates and C.O.s because I was still in a state of delirium. It wasn't long before I went to court and pled guilty to a DUI and got time already served.

I went back to my aunt and uncle's place, and I tried to get my uncle to smoke me out, but he wouldn't and really didn't have to. I found a bud that one of my cousins must have dropped. I smoked it, then I took a nap on their California king-size bed. When I woke up it was time for me to get on the train that took me to D.C., where my dad picked me up.

CHAPTER 10
BACK TO K-TOWN

Now in the story I'm about 19 years of age. I haven't learned a thing or at least haven't yet taken heed of what has been taught to me.

My mom wound up renting a house back in K-town. It was a big house and pretty nice. My room had a balcony, till I traded it for my sister's room which was a much quieter one.

I wasn't there long, though, before I wound up back in jail for disturbing the peace. The police kept coming to my house and straight to my room without even knocking on the door. They would warn me to turn down my music, telling me that it was disturbing the neighbors.

Back in jail, the same things that happened to me during my earlier incarcerations occurred again: Me thinking I was Jesus Christ, then Peter Pan, and then the devil. Then I would start to see visions; I saw a Native American known as Geronimo, who was hovering over the intake desk. He was sitting Indian-style, and he would take a hit from his peace pipe and put his finger over his lips as if he was trying to quiet me or calm me. Soon I was back in the looney bin. This time they kept me there for about three weeks.

When I was released this time, unlike before, I was stable. This time I started going to an outpatient doctor. I had found out a while earlier that I could get high from Benzos like Klonopin and Xanax, and could also make money selling these. So I would go to the doctor and tell the doc that I needed something stronger than Klonopin. I used excuses such as my anxiety was making me not wanting to go into large crowds, or when I got around people I felt like I was going to have a heart attack. Those things were actually somewhat true, but a little exaggerated on my part so as to try and get what I wanted. The doctor wound up giving in until I was up to a script of 90 Xanie bars, which are the highest prescribed dose in the U.S.; they are 2 mgs a pill.

Days went on, and cocaine came and hit K-town pretty hard, maybe harder than ever. I snorted my first line since before the time I went to Louisiana and came back. I also started again flipping pills and trees. I didn't really want to handle cocaine, but it happened anyway. My cousin Jay, B & Lee were the biggest pushers in town, and I so happened to always be around them. Then they would come to my house.

My other people would come in from out of town and set up shop at my cousin's house and also come to mine. We would sometimes do lines and spit rhymes on this stereo I had that had a mic insert and could record.

One day we had a coc gathering, as I call it, just me and all the so-called homies chillin', smoking weed, and snorting coc all night. We probably went through about 1½ or 2 ounces of coc, which I would say was a lot for the eight of us who were in the room.

I wound up going to the bathroom after a line, and my cousin Jay was laid out in the bathroom. He wouldn't reply to me, saying his name, or respond to me hitting his foot. So I just went back into the room and told the rest of the crew that Jay was passed out in the bathroom. They didn't believe me because I was so calm about it. Then they came to realize I was serious and ran into the bathroom. Jay began to laugh and said he was just trying to scare us. None of us thought it was funny, nor had we thought he was joking.

My one cousin was real mad because he wound up spilling his coc. It was like nothing else mattered to us, not our moms, not our dads, not our seed. I guess we took Nas's *kill your mom kill your pop's kill your seed; I'm hustlin' nigga* to the heart. Not literally did we take these words, but we might as well have. We wound up killing everything that mattered, "Love."

I got to the point where I could no longer snort coc, well, at least not for a while. My nasal cavity was eaten up, and every time I would put yayo up there, blood would gush out. One day my cousin Jay sold me a gram for $20.00, which is real cheap being that a g goes anywhere between $80.00 and $100.00 in K-town. I snorted a line and he came on like, "JESUS! Kos, you don't need to snort no more!" as blood gushed out of my nose.

People would always say that if coc made your nose bleed it meant it was good coc, hardly any cut. In some cases that might be true, but not in all.

It came to the point where I learned how to rock it up in a spoon. All you had to do was put the coc in the spoon with a little baking soda, put some water in it, add fire until it got down to where the coc oil was floating on top, then you would take a penny and the crack would stick to the copper of the penny.

CHAPTER 11
NEAR-DEATH EXPERIENCE

Since I started smoking hard, a.k.a. crack cocaine, I was lacing my blunts with it. Jay sold me another gram for $20.00. Then the next day he was going to re-up with some folks across the way. I held onto the gram till the next day. While he was re-n-up, I rocked up and took a blast. My chest was beginning to hurt so I popped aspirin. Then I took another blast till the hard was gone. Then I sat there waiting for Jay to get back from his four-hour trip.

He came back with two onions and laced a blunt, and I started hitting it like it wasn't laced. We were out on my porch and I was like, "Cuz, I need some fresh air."

Jay replied, "We're already outside."

I was like, "Then maybe I need to go inside."

My heart was beginning to speed up, and I could feel the sensation in my chest. I told him to take my pulse. He did, and he just looked at me with the craziest look, and I asked him, "Should I go to the hospital?"

He shook his head yes, still with the craziest look on his face. I wound up getting one of my brother's friends to give me a ride to the hospital. My chest was hurting and I told my sister to pray for me. She could be a bit dramatic sometimes and started freaking out. When we got to the hospital my sister's drama queen skills paid off and she quickly got the attention of a nurse, which would have taken much longer if she hadn't acted dramatic. So I guess being dramatic is cool in some circumstances.

The nurse checked my pulse, and it was 154 beats per minute. I thought I was going to die. One of my brothers stayed in the room with me, and I just kept apologizing for all the times I had been mean to him.

He said, "Stop, apologizing. You're going to be all right."

A doctor came in and asked me what I was on. I told him I had popped a bunch of aspirin and smoked a little weed. At this he got mad and yelled, "Tell me what you were taking!"

My brother stepped in and said, "Don't yell at him. You see he's about to have a heart attack." Just not so nicely was this said, and my bro told me. "Kos, just tell him what you were on."

I told him coc, and the doc gave me some anxiety meds that brought my heart rate down. As soon as my heart rate went down I checked myself out of the hospital. Then I went home and tried to rest. That was the last time I smoked hard or did coc — for a few months, that is. Then like a dummy I was back at it.

I met this girl Trina, and I wish I had never met her. We were together for a few weeks. I felt like I was the man and in all reality she was nothing special, not having the greatest of attitudes. I ask myself what was wrong with me — first Dellilah, now Trina. I had an '89 Old Mobile, and I'd ride back and forth to her apartment. For the first few nights it was all right, with us sexually going at it for hours about seven times a night. You couldn't call me a minute man.

The fun there soon died, though, and I went to perform up at this show opening up for these two local rappers. I just performed one song:

> *"Pain I won't let it drive me insane once again, so I pray to God ask him to catch me cause I feel myself slippin', cuz there's something in this life I'm just not getting, at sixteen I was spitting lyrics just to be rippin' one apart now I wanna see everyone come together for the better. I try to quit dealin', but feins, keep beggin' me not to, Lord please help me to do what is right, I feel so weak in this fight. I barely see any light, I'm struggling hate that I ever started hustlen, destroyin' people so I feel like nothing. Please help me get back to Church where I felt like something, when I go out I*

wanna go out doing good, not by killing everyone in my neighborhood like Akon and Bone I try so hard, but keep getting taken down by misery, bad memory, but I don't want ya to remember me for the bad person I be sometimes I feel there's nothing worse than me. I wanna live, I wanna die, I wanna live, I wanna die.

"The Lord told me let my light shine, but in due time that light would dim, I big not slim, rather live back then when everything wasn't about drugs, now I can't stop drinking while thinking about suicide next time 5-0 is after me, I'm not gonna hide; me and a hollow tip is going to have to collide, but then and I'm a survivor somehow I must survive, been having dreams of getting shot and what not right now, I given you all I got. Sometimes I wanna die, that's why I stay high. I wanna cry, but all my tears have dried up inside. Life's hard, heart scared, I wanna be the best, but before that I see death. I wanna live, but then again, I wanna fly to the heavenly sky where everything will be all right. Lord take me on flight to night. I'd like to see the bright light. I hate myself; I wish I had god health. Wish I never fell in love with a whore, now my brains sore, as well as my heart, dear God, I'm still looking for my fresh start."

Prior to the performance, about a month earlier, my homeboy had gotten coc'd up and xanied up and went and hung himself. He was at my house every day for a few months;

then one day my brother and I were like, "I wonder where Fifs at?" Not much time went by before we got the call. So that song to me is the *Bipolar Soldier Anthem*. I dedicate it to soldiers like Fifty.

After the performance, I went back to Trina's house and knocked on her door, but she didn't answer. She was in there getting her freak on, she told me later. I was stupid and still wanted to be with her. The night she didn't answer the door, I drank about a fifth of E&J and went riding around and wrecked my car. No injuries, thank God, and I wound up avoiding the police; I thought they were going to take me to jail but they just wanted to give me a ticket. So I stayed on the low till they told my mom that if I didn't come down to talk with the officer, there would be a warrant out for my arrest. So I did.

Winston K. Redman

CHAPTER 12
ZOMBIE LAND

Days went on as they do, and I began to pop Xanax and Suboxone. I also began to snort coc a little again and even smoked. I had money in my pocket 95% of the time. I would make trades: Pills for coc, or pills for pills, or even making $5.00 a pill. I also so happened to have another source of income.

Stilts and I would always go to the bar, and he would always say, "I don't have any money."

I'd be like, "You're with me; you know I got you."\

Many nights we would drink till the bar closed. The bartenders loved serving me because I would usually leave a nice tip.

One day Stilts and I were going to the bar starting early, but I so happened to have popped three Xanie bars and a quarter of Suboxone. We stopped at this gas station and I told Stilts I was going to get a drink. The next day he told me he waited outside for 15 minutes before walking in to check on me. He said he had to slap me because I was passed out standing up with the drink door open. I guess I may have been dreaming that I had gotten the drink, paid for it, and left. But who knows? Stilts saw one of my cousins and had him give me a ride back to my house.

I started to really enjoy the high from Xanax and Suboxone. I wound up back down at Dellilah's new place one night, trying to talk to her, and she kept asking if I was all right; she knew I was doped up because I kept nodding in and out. Dellilah and I were just friends at the time. She asked if I needed help getting home, and I was like, "Nah, I'll be all right."

But my addiction had gotten worse and worse, and everyone thought I was going to wind up dead. They were all scared for me.

The house I was living at, with my brothers, mom, and sister, wound up becoming infested with rats and mice, so everyone moved out but me. I stayed for about another month until I found my own place. Before that it was pretty bad, the rats and mice that is. We put poison out everywhere. I remember one day going to get a pair of gloves from under the sink, and there was a rat half-alive, dying from the poison. I just grabbed a hold of it with a bag or something and threw it in the trash. The stench from the rats that were dead and beginning to rot was horrible.

There, just about every time I would go to get into the shower, they would go crazy. These rats weren't your ordinary rats. Have you ever heard of an acrobat? Well, these rats were *acro-rats*. They would make moves that were crazy to get away from my presence — flips, swings, and tightrope walking.

Soon, on TV, I heard about a super-rat invasion. I don't know about super-rats, but they were kind of odd.

I began to go through withdrawals when I would run out of Xanax or Suboxone. I would have nightmares that rats were biting on my chest, and I would hop up out of a dead sleep and be brushing rats off my chest that weren't really there. I even had a nightmare about this rat trying to deceive me by saying, "Come here, I won't eat you." Then he would grab my foot, throw me on the ground, and start gnawing away.

I decided it was about time that I moved.

Winston K. Redman

CHAPTER 13
NEW PLACE

I wound up finding a place across the way. I had met these two girls a while back ago, Molly and Peggy, who lived not too far from me. They would come up and drink with me, smoke bud, and sometimes even crack.

I would pay them to clean my apartment and give me back rubs. I liked one, but she felt that it would be kind of odd if we had gotten together; being that she'd had an affair with my brother in the past. The other, she was cute, but I thought she was just a little too young; but we so happened to party daily. I don't remember too many days when we didn't. The youngest one and her older brother would even stay at my house sometimes, because they were pretty much homeless due to the effects of their dad's crack addiction. Peggy and I became pretty close.

My cousin Lee came over my house one day and had an 8 ball. He hooked me up with some and told me, "If anybody asks where I'm at, don't tell them."

It so happened that I had to go out of town to go make a pick-up of Suboxone. While I was going to the pick-up, Lee's brothers called asking if I knew where he was. I was like, "He's not with me."

They were like, "Don't lie, Kos."

I was like, "I'm not. He's not here." Which he wasn't; he was back at my apartment getting coc'd up.

Later on that day, I went up to their house, and my cousin Thor and I were chillin', then Jay and B came up and were bragging about how they made Lee strip in the middle of the street. It kind of made me sick. Come to find out that Lee had robbed some biker, and Jay and B had to come out of their pockets to make everything cool. Thor said he was leaving and told me to make sure nothing happened to Lee. So I went looking for Lee and found him. He told me how they'd made him strip.

So I went and got one of my homies, Lil' Mickey. Then we found B and I was gonna beat him up and I grabbed him. Major Caine came out with his 9mm cocked and loaded, and told me and Lil' Mickey to get out of his house. I was like, "I'm leaving," as I kept hold of B and dragged him outside.

Then Major Caine and Lil' Mickey wound up scrapping. B and I got into it too, and I hit B in the jaw. Then Lil' Mickey and B fell off the porch, and Jay came down and got in Lil'

Mickey's face. I was close to laying out Jay. Then the woop-woop of a police siren is all I heard, so I took off. Lil' Mickey thinks I left him behind by running from them, but it was the police I was running from because I wasn't trying to go to jail.

That whole night I kept getting threats from B, with him saying they were coming to kick in my door and this and that. If they had, I would have had a slight problem, especially if they would have come in blasting like I thought they would. They were close to Major Caine, and he was fully equipped with semi-autos and autos. And just the day before I had sold my gun to their dad.

When it all went down, I just wound up having to fight Thor, whom I really wasn't trying to fight because I thought of him as the nicest one out of all of them. It so happened to be that was the way the confrontation between us came to a truce. I also called Major Caine and apologized to him for bringing problems to his house.

The cops circled his house all night and he wound up flushing $10,000 worth of work down the toilet, so the story has it.

Thor wound up calling me, telling me he was sorry. I said I was, too, and we said we loved each other. He told me to come up later and he would take me out to eat, and he bought me a bottle of my favorite brandy, E&J. We called E&J *Easus Jesus*.

It wasn't long before Peggy and I came up with the idea of helping each other get off coc and crack. I was still going up to Trina's house and getting some every now and again when I got to feeling lonely. Even messed with her neighbor once in a while; and there was this other girl I messed with once.

Thinking about it now makes me kind of sick, because before I got so far into drugs, I had standards and morals, as I looked for that one I could love and be loved by.

CHAPTER 14
PEGGY AND OUR JOURNEY TOGETHER

So, here are Peggy and I with the idea that we would stop using coc and crack, but we didn't realize we weren't doing much better by what we chose to use instead.

Every day I would go to Peggy's house and roll up enough blunts to get us through the day. Her mom really liked me and saw me as the best friend Peggy ever had, because of my one day bringing her crackers and Ginger Ale when she was feeling sick to her stomach. Anyway, Peggy and I would spend a lot of time together, snorting Xanax and Suboxone. We would also walk around her neighborhood and smoke tree.

Nighttime I found to be the best time. In the middle of the winter the street lights and everywhere we walked seemed like a dream. Didn't really seem real to a certain degree. I guess it wasn't real. We were living a false reality through the drugs, and I was only seeing things how I wanted to see them.

Not having a care in the world, I wound up losing my place and ended up homeless, sleeping on the park bench on the Southside of town. When I woke up I could barely move, because I felt nearly frozen.

Sometimes Peggy's mom didn't mind me staying there. Sometimes I would even go and stay at my mom and dad's because, after being separated for a while, they were back together at the time.

One day I began to lose it — not like hallucinating, but my temper. I would go off on my friends. I would even go off on Peggy, and she didn't really understand what was going on.

I told her, "I'm going back to jail."

She said, "Why do you say that?"

I answered, "I just have that feeling, and when I get that feeling that something like that's going to happen, it happens."

Not even a day later I was up at my dad's, shooting my Berretta 9 replica, and I accidently put a hole in a storage tub my dad was storing things in. Before that I was being kind of stupid, shooting up a Suboxone and some Xanax. Before I primed the Berretta 9 with a CO_2 cartridge, I shot air into my hand to make sure the gun wasn't loaded. And then I went and was messing with my mom and shot air in her face. Nothing different than my dad pointing a real, army-issued 9mm Berretta at me when I was about three. He was playing around, and it was something he probably thought I'd forgotten. Something else he would deny to the grave.

Just like the multiple beatings he gave me every day for a whole school year. Because I was a so-called bad kid, I got those beatings; but I really don't believe I was a bad kid. It was the embarrassment I caused him. Like when I broke my collarbone playing football, and he was embarrassed because I was showing pain and he told me to stop embarrassing him. I always got in trouble because I was an all-out embarrassment to Sergeant First Class Red Dogg.

Anyway, after shooting the hole in his storage tub, he said he was calling the cops. I then put the gun down, which had three BBs in it.

I might have been high, but I wasn't stupid enough to shoot him and get an attempted murder charge filed against me for a BB hitting him above the waist. Instead, we wound up fighting, and this was the second time I fought him and also the last. The Lord God intervened and kept me from snapping his neck. I realized what was about to happen after he had placed both his hands on mine. From the look on his face, I'd say he saw death.

That's something I don't mention much to people. We broke free, and I wound up throwing a rock through one of the windows of his house, and I also slit the tires of his truck. I did three weeks in jail before I lost it and wound up in the looney bin again. As it turned out, I just had to pay for the damages, which I did.

But it grosses me out that I literally had my dad's life in my hands and was about to give his life to God. My dad wound up having to get neck surgery. He says it was from an old football injury, and I think he says that so I don't feel bad, but I think it was my fault. This so happened to eat at me for a very long time, because no matter what my dad ever did to me or how he treated me, he's my dad and I love him. It may not seem like it, but I do forgive him. And like my lil bro Zay says, I made him tough — dad made me tough.

CHAPTER 15
WILL IT EVER END?

After the days I spent in jail and in the looney bin because of me and my dad's altercation, I so happened to move in with my sister and brother. There, I was sleeping on the floor.

One day my brother tried to make me mad, as he usually would do, and kicked me in the head while I was asleep on the floor. I just laid there and didn't say anything, because I knew that if I got up we would have been into another fight. Which brings me back to a time back at the house we were living in that had gotten infested with rats and mice.

FLASHBACK:

A group of us was up partying as usual, doing coc and Xanax, and drinking. I didn't do much that night because I had to go to work the next day. Everyone wound up leaving, and my brother Zay stayed up blasting the TV. After I asked him repeatedly to go to sleep or keep quiet, it finally reached the point where I walked into his room, grabbed his remote, and turned the TV off. There were only certain ways to turn on that specific TV, and it so happened that I made it where he couldn't turn it back on without the remote. So, Zay began throwing things, and I ran back into his room, slammed him up against the wall, and told him to just go to sleep. He wound up swinging on me, so I drilled him in his jaw. He went running down the stairs out of the house. Next thing you know, rocks started flying through the windows; it looked like Iraq before they got their high-powered slingshots.

I wound up going to the kitchen, and right when I was at the door a boulder went flying past me. I was like, "I ain't putting up with this," and I ran outside with a broomstick and hit him. It just wrapped around him because it was aluminum. So I wound up trying to knock him out, but due to the effects of the drugs he was on, he didn't go down. He wound up breaking free and went and got a knife from his best friend, who lived across the street. I found out about that later. My sister wound up calling the cops, something I couldn't ever bring myself around to doing. I went back to the kitchen and saw him run by; then I saw a cop chasing him. He spent the day in jail to have time to sober up.

Anyway, while living with my brother and sister, I kept smoking weed and even got back into crack. Jay and I would go to this place out of town and get high with this old guy who would be considered by some as a "hillbilly." He looked like one of those guys on *Duck Dynasty*. We would go there or other places.

Peggy and I stopped hanging out because she found a boyfriend, and while I was locked up she didn't have any supply of Xanax or Suboxone and started having seizures. She had to get put on Klonopin. She is now married with kids. Last I spoke to Peggy, she said how she would always talk about me with her new friends she would come across.

I wasn't out long before I wound up back in jail. I was up for days on coc and started hallucinating. I thought the apartment of my cousin's girlfriend was mine, and wound up getting a B&E charge for it. Thank God those charges were dropped.

Eventually I got myself back together, got out, and my mom helped me find another apartment, where I lived for about two or three years.

During my first few months in my new apartment, not much went on, just smoking tree and a little drinking. My cousin Thor and I started to hang pretty tight. He started dating this girl, Penny, whom I knew from back in middle school. Back then, I'd had a crush on Penny, but she would never give me the time of day. Thor found it in his heart never to leave me hanging if he went to stay at her house, which was a little ways out of town, so I would be with him.

At one time Penny had lived right across the street from me. That was back when we were in middle school. Penny wound up having a kid with my homeboy Caine. They were always back and forth, together and happy one day, then she was throwing his clothes into the dumpster the next. That was before her and Thor came to be. Penny and Thor wound up moving about five blocks down from me, so we were constantly hanging out at their place.

It came to be that we would party pretty much every day. We made sure we always had smoke; if they didn't have it, I had it. We drank, snorted yayo, and I was back on Suboxone. Some nights we would play poker. That's where I became pretty bad at gambling, always going bar-hopping, and hitting up the machines for quick come-ups which rarely happened.

One night, Penny and her friend Lilly were sitting in this ride. While Thor was inside, Penny was like, "Look, Kos."

I turned and looked into the back seat.

Penny said, "Don't tell Thor," and wound up making out with Lilly.

Thor got back in the ride, and we went back to their crib. This one dude from out of town, whom I didn't know, was there with us. Anyway, Penny and Lilly began having whipped cream fights. Lilly said she was going up to take a shower and told Penny to come up with her and said, "Kos's the only one that can come with us." So I went. Before I did, I was trying to find a rubber, but couldn't find one.

When I got upstairs, Penny was buck-naked, running around, and she said, "Hurry up, Kos." But there was a slight problem I was having, a VD outbreak. So Penny and Lilly wound up in the shower together. Lilly stuck her tail feather out like *Get it, Kos*. But I couldn't because I was afraid to spread what I had been having an outbreak of; I definitely wasn't trying to smash without a rubber because the disease would surely have spread.

A few weeks later, I tried to smash off Lilly, but she was like, "I don't give people second chances." My homeboy Tank, R.I.P., wound up with her that night.

FLASHBACK:

Tank and I always bumped heads about stupid things, but he was a cool dude.

One day, he wound up trippin' on mushrooms and got scared and called the police on himself. Tank wound up getting stabbed to death about a year or so later. One day before that had occurred, he bought a pistol. He and I were sitting, smoking a blunt, and I told him, "Put three in the air for me when I ain't here."

He was like, "You know I got you, but you ain't going nowhere."

Now he's gone.

Well, the days of partying went on. I wasn't doing much Snow or crack at this time. Thor, B, Lee, and Jay were, though. I wish I would have found a new group of people to hang with.

I started hanging with these Italians, one of whom always wanted me to get him yayo, and he would always ask me to take trips with him out of town. That's one thing I didn't do.

He would say, "There's a lot of money to get," and I thought about it. What he wanted me to do was be a driver, delivering coc from this spot to that spot. I wasn't to touch anything. He would say, "Just take the car, make the drop-off, and take the clean car." But I didn't go for it.

One night he showed me his new piece — a chromed-out pistol. He was the kind of guy who would invite me over to eat on Thanksgiving with him and the rest of his family and girlfriend. The night he showed me the gun, I was at his house because he wound up getting a hook-up. Then began to flip. So, I was there to purchase. The day after, I had him come meet me, and had my cousin B hop in the ride, grab the drugs, hop out, and run. All we got was an 8-ball. An 8-ball that almost cost me my life.

Two days later the Italian was down at the bottom of my stairs knocking on the door. I expected it to be him, so, I didn't answer; I just went and looked out my window and saw his truck parked in front of my friend's house. Then I saw him take off.

But the next night he caught up with me at this store. He had a mean look on his face and told me to come to him. With his broken-up English-Italian accent he said, "You're lucky you didn't open your door last night."

I was like, "Why, were you going to shoot me?"

He was like, "Yeah!"

I said, "It wasn't my fault."

He was like, "Don't worry about it, just come by later."

Well, I was dumb enough to go. Luckily nothing bad happened, but when I look back on it now I see it as a dumb move. I just wound up bringing him $2,000 in one night. Thor and one of our homeboys, Crackle, kept sending me up there for grams.

That's all the Italian would sell. He did sell one ball, but after that just grams. So I was in and out of his place about 18 times through the night. Crackle was the one buying; he would give me a little out of each bag to free base off foil. Then he and Thor would rock up the rest. The night eventually came to an end. Thor and Crackle left. I went to the store, bought some scratch-offs, won $50 off those dollar tickets, then went and bought a half-gram and went home and free based it. Then tried to calm down and go to sleep. So I could wake up and chase my high all over again.

Though I had almost gotten shot for robbing the Italian, that didn't stop me, B, Lee, Jay, or Thor from plotting schemes, day to day, for ways to come up with money without having any dope to sell. What we would do is make dummy bags, and people fell for those dummy bags every time. It was crazy.

Sometimes Jay and I would go to the extreme of acting like we didn't know each other. I'd be the dealer, and he would be in the ride with customers wanting heroin. We'd have Quick chocolate milk mix in aluminum foil. I would wait for him to call me, then I would meet him somewhere.

He'd be like, "You got the goods?"

I'd be like, "Yeah."

He would give me the money and I would give him the Quick chocolate milk mix. I'd get a percentage and he would also. We also made dummy bags of coc from flower, and that was another way we'd get people; and we'd sell candle wax as crack. Ripping off people went back to when I sold parsley or even grass from the bottom of my lawn mower.

Drugs are stupid and make you be stupid.

CHAPTER 16
VAIN GAME OF STUPIDITY CONTINUES TO REMAIN

Nights and days I would get high. It would usually be around 5:00 in the morning before I would walk home to crash. On my walks, I would always talk to Jesus Christ. Being hearing-impaired due to the drugs, and always talking, never was I open to listening to what He was trying to tell me through other people. I sometimes wondered if people would see me and think I was crazy. You all who know me and are reading this are probably like, "No, we know you were." I slept with my Bible, and opened it up pretty much every day to read at least one Scripture.

I was seeking help that I couldn't receive because I was serving two masters, drugs and God, and was trying to bow down to them both, which doesn't work. So, I continued putting smoke in the air and never putting the pill or liquor bottle down, and that's when I became a bummed-out clown.

Holes in my clothes and my shoes, my feet stinking, my hair growing, my beard never shaved — me just looking straight rugged. I mean, I would go like two to three days without showers at times.

Later I got a little better about keeping up with myself. I'd say that time was worse than the time I went AWOL from Juvy with another inmate and slept in a dumpster to stay warm. I'd say that because I had running water, and money that I blew as ashes. I had the choice to shower and buy nice clothes and things. The family of one of my friends didn't have those great luxuries, though, and would at times ask to use my shower, so they wouldn't have to keep filling their tub with boiled water to keep the tub water warm. Things I took for granted.

Penny and I, though, came to be pretty close. When Thor wasn't around, she and I would take pleasure in each other's company in a friendly way. You know I had feelings for her, and at times I would let her know this, but she was too stuck on Thor.

Nights would go by that Thor would leave and wouldn't come back, and she hated staying at her place by herself, especially if her son was at his grandma's place, so she would ask me to stay. I would stay up in her son's bed, and she in hers.

She asked me about three times to stay, but I only did so once. The night I did stay she ran in the room and just hugged me, as I sat up to her. She just held me tight, thanking me for being her friend and for not being like Thor's brothers, who would always try to get in her drawers. I mean, I wanted Penny and I know I could have had her.

A few times I asked her if she wanted to get a car so just she and I could ride away. She said yes the first time I asked her. The second time I asked she said, "Kos, why ask me when I already told you?" I was to out of it, by the enchantment cast on me by witch doctors from South America, to be her knight in shining armor. She wanted love as I wanted love.

Thor was also overtaken by the enchantments of the South American witch doctors, and he would try to tell me about how he forgot how to love and how everyone was seeking God and couldn't find Him. I told Thor I would go and find God and bring Him back to him. I did find God, but have not yet had the opportunity to bring Him back to Thor. In all reality, I hope Thor forgot about my search and went on to find Jesus Christ for himself. But if he hasn't, then I still plan to bring God back to him.

My cousin Taz and his girlfriend Dafny wound up moving in with me. They were a trip, always fighting. They stayed with green and kept me high. They never paid their portion of the rent, but they kept me high. That I saw as all right payment at the time. They were good company. Taz, I tried to get him to keep the people he was bringing to the house at a minimum — and no one but him was ever, ever, ever, ever, allowed in my room. He didn't listen, though; he had his whole squad chillin' every day. The squad, I don't speak of; they were none of my business, really. Although it was like every team wanted me on theirs.

My team was T.S.O.B.S., which stands for Tears Shed Over Blood Shed. Mainly this was just all about pouring liquor out, while the rest of the colors were about shedding blood. I was about spreading love and would recommend fighting only when absolutely necessary. When Pinky and the Brain were thinking of taking over the world, I was thinking the same — and what better way to do it than with love?

CHAPTER 17
TRYIN' TO FOCUS

Taz and Dafny would also always be at Thor and Penny's. Partying went on there nonstop. I would usually wake up, go knock on Thor's door, we would smoke, and then go on with our day. Many days I would walk up to B and Lee's after smoking with Thor. Usually, I would be plotting a way to make money. After leaving there, I would usually wind up in the Projects. If I had pills, that's usually where I would wind up, at Aladdin's setting up shop. I would have him call people who were looking, wait a while, make a few sells, then be out.

Sometimes I would stay up there, and get drunk and high with Aladdin and his mom's boyfriend. Even at times when Aladdin wasn't there, I would stay and chill with his mom's boyfriend. Before winding up there, I would stop at everyone else's house on the way up, letting people know I was good if they needed anything and giving them my number, which I always changed. Then I would stop at B and Lee's, and from there, the Projects. Later I would usually be back at Thor and Penny's.

Nights would get wild there at times — everyone drinking, smoking, popping E, and snorting coc. E was one thing I tried to stay away from. I didn't even really want to handle it, because I knew eventually I would have started popping it.

I didn't have to go to the strip club; it would have been a waste. A waste because I had Lilly stripping for me all the time. One night, when I got my first lap dance, Lilly was doing her thing. She went and tried to do a handstand and shake her tail feathers and just fell over. I couldn't help but laugh. There you would see girls on girls and every other corrupt thing under the sun. I would say that at that time I wasn't too far from the land of Sodom and Gomorrah.

Days like this went on for months. One night Thor got me some shrooms, first time I tripped off them. I tripped off Acid and Robitussin and Coricidin Cough & Cold, which is called "Robo Trippin" and "Skittling/Triple c's." The Triple c's looked like Skittles, so it's obvious how the trip got called "Skittling."

The shrooms were more intense and I so happened to think for days they opened my mind to all the knowledge known to man and even God. Taz and Dafny also tripped that night. I tripped for three days after that day, with my homeboy Convict. After that, Thor and I started going at it, my feelings for Penny growing with my trip. I didn't sleep for days, and Halloween was a wild night.

Winston K. Redman

CHAPTER 18
WILL I EVER MAKE IT BACK?

Things started getting crazy with Taz, Dafny, and the squad. So I told them they had to go. Taz would have Dafny hollering and screaming due to the simple fact that she was half-nuts. While he would walk away after an argument, she would chase him down in her car, begging him not to leave. I think it's possible she wasn't too different from Doctor Jekyll and Mr. Hyde.

One day we were up at the bowling alley. Taz and I were talking business and Dafny got tired of us talking. While Taz had one foot out of the ride, she took off. He flew out of the ride doing flips, and she stopped the car, saying how sorry she was. Taz wound up punching out the window. That's how crazy things were getting between the two. After that, Dafny wound up moving out, and Taz stayed at my place.

My birthday came around, and I had started early with a bottle of E&J I'd had in the freezer for about a month. Penny, Thor, B, Lee, Tank, Jay, and I drank from the time we were up until I went home that night. Penny and I started earlier than the rest on the shots. Tank, Penny, and I then went to the bar, and she wound up getting barred for throwing a cigarette at the bartender. My night ended with me going back to my place, where I walked into the kitchen and saw this girl I knew, Jasmin (Aladdin's ex), walking around and cooking in my kitchen buck-naked. There I was thinking Taz had a surprise for me, although I really wasn't wanting it to come from her. Come to find out, he'd just had a little shindig going on there for himself.

He made me mad because he let his friend into my room, which I had just cleaned, and everything was kind of out of place. Also, someone had been in my bed sexing. Not when I came in, but I knew what had happened because of the clothes that were all around my bed. I was pretty heated, ready to kick Taz out, but I didn't. However, he wound up leaving anyway, moving in with this chick from the next town over.

Before Thor and I started bumping heads, Thor introduced me to this hippie who always kept good green. There are all kinds of good green, but you just have to know where to find it. So-called good green would be all sorts of different strains and which had all sorts of different names. All the bud I smoked that I could remember was Chocolate Tye; Beasters; Northern Lights; Granddaddy Purp; Blueberry; Orange Haze; Sage; Sour Apple Diesel; Hydro Cinderella;

Purple Haze; Emerald Wonder; G-1 Lemon, which was medical; and my all-time favorite, Kush.

Anyway, after meeting this hippie I would be at his house every day during harvest season. Harvest season is in October, which is the best time to get the best bud. He was over-pricing a little — $60.00 an eighth, which usually goes for $50.00. By this time, though, you should know that didn't stop me. He had some good that had neon pink hairs going through it, and if you're a pot smoker or use to be, you know what I mean by hairs. I would smoke mainly by myself, smoking out of this glass piece which was chip-free. I started really losing it, though, after the shroom trip.

I would go to Thor's and start talking trash on him, trying to tell Penny she should leave him and just come with me. I would say stuff like, "He's a fake, good-for-nothing bum."

I think Thor might have known that I was losing it because he wouldn't say anything, and Thor — well, if he'd wanted to — he could have easily laid down the hammer.

Penny would just laugh and say, "I don't know where all this is coming from."

I could tell her now it was from a mind fried; it couldn't have been from the heart. I mean, Thor and I would have moments where we would basically cry on each other's shoulders. I had much love for my cousin. I know it may seem like I'm trying to justify the situation and my actions, but I was out of my mind.

I soon met up with an old friend, Money. He and I went back a ways; he, Lil' Mickey, and I used to chill on the regular back in our teen years. Money's brother and I wound up into it, though Money and I were straight. It seemed like every time I would be at Money's or see him, it wasn't long before I was back in jail for something stupid. I went and scored some dope at Money's from his other brother. Then I was going to try and take a trip out of my mind to the city to get a big amount of yayo. That didn't happen.

The next day I went to Money's, and his brother whom I had a problem with was there. He started threatening me, saying that he was going to kill me. A few days earlier, I had put a "Mayweather" on him.

He was Taz's mom's boyfriend and I would let them use my credit card. Before that, Dice, Money's brother, stole me in the jaw for telling him that his product wasn't good. Then the next day we shook hands. Then, I owed Taz's mom some money for something, so I gave her my card and told her that I needed it back by tomorrow. When I went to get it, Dice wound up giving me a hard time about it. I got the card and spent all the money on it. I owed them a little money off of it. I told him when he gave it back, "It's not like I was going to rob you." So after the money was spent, I went on avoiding Dice, until one day I walked by Taz's aunt's house, where Dice was standing.

Dice came up on me like, "Kos, where's my money?"

I was like, "You'll get your money when I feel like getting it to you."

Dice replied, "What do I look like, a chump to you?"

I was like, "Nah, I didn't say that."

I then caught him with a right hook. He grabbed a hold of my shoulder and I so happened to drill him a few more times. He said, "Let me go," and I did.

As Dice walked away he said, "I'm gonna kill you, I put it on my daughter, I'm gonna kill you."

Because he'd put it like that, I figured his words were written in stone. So I ran home, grabbed my blade, and some clothes. Then I went to Thor's and laid low because the cops had been called. This all happened before my and Thor's altercation.

I got some money, and bought a BB gun; in case Dice came at me with the real deal, I would be able to use it for some kind of defense. Thor and I went to the gambling spot, and Taz's mom and Dice were there as they always were.

Taz's mom began yelling at me like, "Where's my money at, Kos? That's wrong what you did in front of my niece."

She was getting off the bus when Dice and I got into it. So, I got a little bass in my voice, started cussing, and said, "Don't go there with me." I went to my pocket, pulled out a wad of cash, and gave her the $8.00 I owed her.

She was like, "$8.00?"

I was like, "Yeah, $8.00," as I hit the machine button in aggravation.

Dice came in, she gave him the $8.00, and he said, "Kos, you straight with me," then he put his words on his daughter. I didn't have to worry about anything from him, at least right then.

After the falling out with me and Thor, I kept going over to Money's. Dice was there one day, and he began to start his threats again. The reason being is that he walked in the room after I yelled at his girl, Taz's mom. He kept saying he was going to kill me, and I was like, "Go ahead, kill me, be what you say you're about."

He was like, "You're gonna make me have to go back to NY."

I was like, "Do what you're gonna to do, I'm ready to die."

I was losing it, no sleep, and Dice considered me food on a plate.

Winston K. Redman

CHAPTER 19
HIGH SPEED CHASE

It came to be I was tripping so bad from everything going on, my mind fried and delusional, that I robbed my own mother by stealing her car. Fleeing, I crossed over into another state. The fact that I robbed my mom haunts me to this day, especially when I remember the look of fear I saw on her face as I was stealing her car.

While in the other state, I wound up getting involved in a high-speed chase, being pursued by the cops, during which I was at times driving on the wrong side of the road, dodging other cars. I even almost sideswiped a bus. Thank God I didn't. I'd say that God has always, from day one, had His hand on me. He sure did that day.

The cops and I wound up on a straight stretch of road, and they came up right beside me, I'm sure ready to shoot. Fear hit me hard when I looked into their car. They wound up boxing me in, and I pulled over and stopped.

The cops at the ready with their guns drawn, I got out of the car. Immediately they threw me to the ground, handcuffed me, and threw me into the back seat of one of the cop cars.

During the chase, while I was driving, I was listening to this song, "I'll meet you half way, right up the border line." I was so delusional, I thought I was going to meet a girl while on my way to, I don't know where, straight to the jail cell, I guess. I did meet a pretty C.O. in jail, though.

While in the jail, I wound up getting into it with this gang-banger, then ended up in the Hole for 25 days. While in there, I cussed at the C.O.s. They didn't like me too well, and they hit me with some pepper spray twice, which got me more time in the Hole. I ended up spending more than 112 days in the Hole, until my extradition.

I was then sent to another jail, where I met up with this dealer from K-town. He wound up being my cellmate. There was this one dude whose nose I broke because he called my homeboy a nigger. This left him dripping blood up the hall on the way to medical.

It wasn't long before I bailed myself out. Before I did, I didn't think I was going to get out for a while. So I called Lee and told him to break into my apartment, get a few of my things, and keep them safe. He went in and got everything that was worth money: My bowl, a $300.00 throwback jersey, and my Jordans. But he didn't get any of the things I told him to get.

My bowl got sold, which is okay. But my cousin from the Cacalacis had given me the jersey, and B told me he put it up for me. I heard Jay wound up getting a hold of it and sold it for a cap of heroin that was only in all reality worth nothing but a street value price of $5.00 to $10.00 or your life.

God bless the ones suffering from the life of drugs. And here let me offer a word to the wise: Is the drug life really worth our lives? Our lives are not our own, after all, but are everyone's who loves us, as well as God's.

I'm sorry to everyone who watched me in my struggle, making it a part of their own struggles, and I speak on behalf of all of us addicts: We need help; please do everything you can to help us.

Winston K. Redman

CHAPTER 20
LAST CHANCE

Now I had reached the point in my life where I thought I'd make a slight effort to change — but my effort was too slight. I had bailed myself out of jail and I wound up in college. I didn't make it through and graduate, however, but I felt proud of myself just because I was sitting somewhere I thought I would never or could ever be.

Unfortunately, my self-discipline soon came to an end. Marijuana, coc, heroin, Suboxone, Hydrocodone, percs, Xanax, Klonopin, Oxycontin, inhalants, Ritalin, Adderol, and alcohol. Day in and day out, for years, I've done these drugs, each time shooting the possibility of death into my veins. That I've seen enough of, I guess, to make me stop doing it and never return to it again. It seems the ones who always OD'd did so due to firing up.

I so happened to find myself in the same position I once had been, or maybe simply had never really gotten myself out of. cocaine I would do all through the summer. Thor and I started hanging again, but Penny, well, she wasn't too fond of me anymore. While in jail, I had kept writing her letters — letters that were crazy love letters. She didn't want to chill, just me and her, anymore, as we had before.

I'd ask her to smoke, and she would say she was good. I and Thor's kids, Penny's kids and B's kids were pretty close. I felt something like an uncle to them, although, I was just their big cousin.

I would ask Thor's oldest what video game he wanted, then I would tell him, "I'm not going to make promises but I'll try and have it here by next week at this time." So, I went and got the new *Ninja Turtle* game he wanted and the *G.I Joes* that Penny's kids wanted; and would have to say that it's the best feeling in the world to give things to kids who appreciate it.

I was also trying to get B's son gold coins every month so he could collect them, which I did; but I didn't stay out long enough to get him the collection I was wanting to give him. He and I seemed the closest. I miss boxing with him; he was good competition for a three-year-old, with a killer left hook.

As the days went on, however, I was drifting further and further beyond reality. I was introduced to this guy, Big Apple, and I made one trip with him. He wanted me to start moving yayo for him, so I did. I told him I wouldn't mess it up, but with coc you never know what is going to happen. I started chilling with this chick, Ireland, while I was flipping, never even hit it. We would kiss sometimes, but she played hard-to-get; and she was just there for my coc and pills anyway.

When I started with Ireland I kept messing things up, so I messed up Big Apple's money. I thought he was going to kill me, but it was only $100.00 I owed him. Some people can get serious about their money, but Big Apple was one you could work with. I took a trip with him and B, and we got some yayo. I found him the ride, so I asked if he would spot me for that; he did. I gave him my word that I wouldn't mess up that ball, but it came to where I messed up a $3,000.00 loan.

I liked hustling, but that was the dark side of me. My cousin's girl, I met about five times a day, serving her whatever she wanted. As dangerous as it was, I found it just as fun.

I wound up even copping some from my homeboy, Money, and his was better than usual for once. I, Big Apple, Mali Mal, and two chicks, Mini and Starlite, wound up at a strip club. Starlite kept asking me if she could get a line off of me or spot her a half-gram. So, I asked her, "Can I come stay with you tonight?"

She said, "Yeah, just don't' tell Big Apple."

I had to make sure with Big Apple that he wouldn't be mad if I was to get with her. He said he didn't care. I mean, he shouldn't have been mad because he already had a girl. A month prior to this, I told Lee, after walking back to his house, that I could picture her riding me. Starlite and I kept up doing coc until we wound up back at her place. I wanted her bad, so I didn't have sex with her; I made love. For about three hours love-making went on. She was on top for some time, just as I had told Lee I had pictured.

CHAPTER 21
"LORD, I DON'T WANNA DIE LIKE THIS"

I was wanting Starlite, but the same feelings weren't the ones I was getting back from her. Our fling was what it was; the drugs clouded my mind too much for me to know what a true relationship was. To tell the truth, I still don't know what a true relationship is.

There were days she would tell me she wanted to chill with me. She would tell me to meet her after work, and I'd be waiting. Then, she'd hop in another car. Starlite was very bad on my emotions. It's cool now; I mean, I should have known better.

Zay and I became a little closer; I would try to party with him and take him out to eat and things. I missed him when he got sent to Iraq, so when he arrived back I was happy. One day, I asked him to let me hold his weapon. I was planning on getting at the dude who had robbed me at Dellilah's place about four or five years earlier, since he had just gotten out of prison.

Zay said, "If you're gonna do that, I hope you enjoy that hat your wearing, 'cause it'll be the last time you're gonna wear that hat. I hope you enjoy that pizza, 'cause that's the last time you're gonna eat that pizza." With that he continued talking and I listened, but taking what he was saying to heart was a different story.

I then tried to get Big Apple to let me hold his weapon, telling him I didn't have anything to live for, as we were sitting down at this Chinese restaurant.

He just said, "You're crazy."

So it came to be that I didn't put the burner to the dude who had robbed me.

One day, Starlite came up to my house because she wanted to get some pain pills off me because she had kidney stones. She said we could chill later if I wanted, and I said all right, looking forward to it like a dummy. I told her I was going out of town and that I'd call her when I got back. I tried calling, I tried texting, but nothing. So I figured I would rock up the coc I had gotten for her and I to chill on.

I felt alone and close to death. So, as I got to my last few blasts of crack, I prayed to God, telling Him: "Lord, I don't wanna die like this. Somehow, some way, Lord Jesus, let me get back to being close to you, again. Even if I end up going back to jail or the looney bin, please spare me another near-death experience, because they don't work for me."

As I finished my prayer, I kind of did not think too much more about the prayer. Instead, I went into my room, popped 50 Klonopins, snorted half a Suboxone, and ate about 5 Risperdals, hoping never to wake up again.

But wake up I did.

Winston K. Redman

CHAPTER 22

RETALIATION THAT HAPPENED

The night went by, then morning came and I made it alive. A lot of people said I should have died from the 50 Klonopins alone, but I didn't. Instead, I got out of bed, took a shower, got dressed, and went up to B and Lee's.

When I got up there they were in the bathroom, probably smoking. I saw they had Suboxone lines laid out, as they did every morning. There were three of the lines, so I was going to do one and give it back to them later.

Being that I had some at my apartment, Lee came out of the bathroom like, "Kos, what are you doing?"

I said, "I was going to do a line and pay you back."

He was like, "You're tryin' to rob us."

I was like, "All the things I do for you, and I'm going to try and rob you?"

He said, "So what?" and punched me in the nose.

B came around the corner and began punching me in the ribs. Then both of them ripped my key chain off my neck and ran my pockets.

I was like, "Let me get my keys and I'll be out."

B said, "Let him get his keys, so he can leave."

Lee was like, "That's why you just got your @*$ beat."

I was like, "I'm gonna get my gun."

Lee said, "Go get your gun." as he hit me again.

I pushed him. Then remember getting ready to leave and blacking out.

I woke up at the bottom of the hill with people yelling, "Get off him or I'll the call the cops!"

B and Lee were like, "Call the cops," and were cussing them.

This lady asked me if I needed a ride. I asked her if she could take me to my apartment. She kept insisting that I go to the hospital because it looked like my nose was broken, and it was possible I had suffered a concussion as a result of how bad they had been stomping me. I asked her to just take me to my house. The cops were called, I heard, but didn't show up until twenty minutes after the incident had occurred.

Back at my apartment, I went to wash the blood off my face, put some different clothes on, loaded my gun, and went looking for B and Lee. Instead, I ran into one of my homeboys, and he so happened to calm me down. So I figured I would just go home and sleep it off.

But as I was walking Thor and Lee were coming from the direction of my apartment, and Thor had a boulder in his hand. I pulled out my gun, a P119-mm Tek, and fired two shots. They took off running. I then took off in the opposite direction. When I got to the end of the road, a cop hollered, "Freeze or I'll shoot!"

I took off running and ran into this business building, where I tried to hide in the bathroom. I soon went to walk out and the same cop said, "Come out or I'll shoot!" I thought for a second, then wound up walking out. More cops yelled, "Get on the ground! Get on the ground!" As I was getting on the ground, a cop came up and threw me to the ground and put an M-16 to my head, telling me, "If you make one move I will blow your head off."

I was charged with six counts of Attempted Murder and six counts of Wanton Endangerment.

Winston K. Redman

CHAPTER 23
IS THIS THE END?

Going through my head now are my years of incarceration. The times I spent using drugs and chasing my high. The times in Juvy going AWOL, fighting to survive, learning the appropriate time to stand up for myself and not be a pushover. Fighting off rapists, protecting my food tray like a dog that would snap on you if you tried to take it away. The torment the C.O.s would inflict upon me while I was going through my hallucinations and delusions. Thinking about how I could of gone somewhere with my life. Thinking of how I should have listened to the ones who tried to lead me in the right direction, the ones who I instead ignored.

Also going through my head now is how sorry I am for the pain I brought to my family. I also remember the stories my uncles would tell about their own times inside prison walls.

I ask myself these questions now: Will I make it? Do I have what it takes to make it? Will I do what I have to do to make it?

My Uncle T once said, "It doesn't matter how big you are or how tough you are, it's almost impossible for anybody to make it through those prison walls." He said that after doing 16 years in a maximum security prison.

So here I am, on my first day back in jail, with all of these thoughts running through my mind — as well as the thought that I don't want to live.

With that thought in mind, I begin to contemplate suicide. I decide to do it. To that end, I go into my cell, get a sheet, tie it to the top-tier rail in the POD, thinking my life is already over and that I may as well jump.

So I tie the sheet around my neck, with the words "Just do it" running through my head.

I make a successful jump over that rail.

But, well, you know what they say: "Saints Live Forever."

CPSIA information can be obtained
at www.ICGtesting.com
Printed in the USA
FFOW04n0554240315
12101FF